# ZIGGY
## and the
# MOONLIGHT
### SHOW

D0100414

To Mum - K.L.

**SIMON & SCHUSTER**
First published in Great Britain in 2018 by Simon & Schuster UK Ltd
1st Floor, 222 Gray's Inn Road, London, WC1X 8HB • A CBS Company
Text and illustrations copyright © 2018 Kristyna Litten • The right of Kristyna Litten
to be identified as the author and illustrator of this work has been asserted by her in
accordance with the Copyright, Designs and Patents Act, 1988 • All rights reserved,
including the right of reproduction in whole or in part in any form • A CIP catalogue
record for this book is available from the British Library upon request.
978-1-4711-4579-7 (HB) • 978-1-4711-4580-3 (PB) • 978-1-4711-4581-0 (eBook)
Printed in China • 10 9 8 7 6 5 4 3 2 1

KRISTYNA LITTEN

# ZIGGY
and the
# MOONLIGHT
SHOW

**SIMON & SCHUSTER**
London   New York   Sydney   Toronto   New Delhi

Ziggy loved Saturdays. All week long she looked forward to the spectacular Moonlight Show.

But this Saturday, her dreams of the day ahead were interrupted by a loud . . .

"HOO HOO!"

Ziggy knew it was no ordinary call.
This bird had lost her chick.

"Don't worry," said Ziggy.
"I can help."

"If she has black and white stripes like you and me, she'll be easy to find and we'll be back in time for the show!"

They hadn't travelled far before . . .

"Achooo!"

Something landed with a tickle on Ziggy's nose.

It was a small, stripy beetle.

"It's going towards the lake," said Ziggy.
"Maybe we'll find your chick there."

When they reached the water's edge,
Ziggy spotted something.

"Look! Stripy feathers in the reeds."

"HOO HOO,"
Bird called.

"Ribbit, ribbit," croaked some feasting frogs.

Ziggy laughed.

"Let's keep looking."

"There!" Ziggy said, as they reached a clearing in some silvery trees. "I can see something black and white in the branches."

"HOO HOO,"

called Bird.

# "Grrrrrrrrrr,"

yawned a tiger.

"Eeeek," whispered Ziggy.
And she and Bird wandered on in the hot sun.

Just as they were about to rest . . .

"Stripes!" Ziggy shouted.
"Your chick is hiding in the grass."

"HOO HOO,"
called Bird.

# "Sssssssssssss,"

hisssssssed a snake,

flicking his tongue

between his fangs.

## "Aaarghhhh!"
shouted Ziggy and Bird.

They found themselves
in a gloomy wood.

"I'm sorry," Ziggy said. "I've been no help at all
and now we'll miss the show."
But Bird had fluttered to the treetops.

But amongst all the other birds'
chirps and chitters, she could
hardly be heard.

Bird needed help.
So Ziggy took a deep breath.

"HOO
HOO
HOO!"

they bellowed together.

And the wood fell silent.

Until out of the stillness
came a tiny,

"Poe!
Poe!
Poe!"

And down through the branches
hopped the little chick.

"We did it!" cheered Ziggy. "Come on, if we hurry we might get home in time for the Moonlight Show."

"Hoo! Poe!" chirped the birds.

But Ziggy had no idea which way their home was.
Everything looked different in the dark.

At last she spotted the scaly snake.
They snuck around him quietly.
He didn't seem so scary now.

"If the snake is here, we'll reach
the silvery trees if we keep going
this way," Ziggy said.

Sure enough, they soon came across the snoozy tiger.

And there were the greedy frogs resting their full bellies.

Burp!

Croak!

Ziggy, Bird and Chick raced
to the place where they watched
the show every week.

Were they too late?

Suddenly Ziggy heard a rustle . . .

and a flurry of moths appeared,
swirling around the stars.

The animals watched
the show for hours.

And when the last moth had fluttered away,
they settled down together, already looking
forward to the next Saturday night.